Runaway

AN
ORCA
YOUNG
READER

Runaway

Becky Citra

ORCA BOOK PUBLISHERS

National Library of Canada Cataloguing in Publication Data
Citra, Becky

Runaway / Becky Citra.

"An Orca young reader"

ISBN 1-55143-276-5

I. Title.

PS8555.I87R86 2003   jC813'.54   C2003-910880-5

PZ7.C499Ru 2003

Library of Congress Catalog Card Number: 2003107507

Summary: Max and Ellie series. Historical fiction. Max must face his first moral dilemma when an abused boy turns up in his secret fort in the forest.

Teachers' guide available at www.orcabook.com

Orca Book Publishers gratefully acknowledges the support of its publishing programs provided by the following agencies: the Department of Canadian Heritage, the Canada Council for the Arts, and the British Columbia Arts Council.

Cover design by Christine Toller
Cover illustration by Don Kilby
Interior illustrations by Stephen McCallum
Printed and bound in Canada

Orca Book Publishers is proud to demonstrate its commitment to the responsible use of our natural resources. This book is printed on Bioprint Paper supplied by Transcontinental Printing. Bioprint paper is 100% recycled, 100% post-consumer waste, processed chlorine-free, 100% Ancient-Forest free, and acid-free, using soy based inks.

IN CANADA	IN THE UNITED STATES
Orca Book Publishers	Orca Book Publishers
1030 North Park Street	PO Box 468
Victoria, BC Canada	Custer, WA USA
V8T 1C6	98240-0468

05 04 03 • 5 4 3 2 1

For the boys and girls at
Bridge Lake Elementary School

CHAPTER ONE

"Stay in the wagon with your sister, Max," said Papa.

"But Papa ... "

Papa picked his way through the weeds to Sam Black's cabin. He knocked on the door and then disappeared inside.

Sam Black and his boy had moved here a month ago. You could see where Sam Black had started to cut down a few trees to clear a field and then given up. The bottom step of the cabin was missing and an old broken wagon wheel lay in the weeds. A huge brown bull stared at us over a rickety fence, munching on a mouthful of grass.

We'd passed by the cabin once before and I'd heard someone shouting, but I'd never even had a glimpse of Sam Black or his boy. It wasn't fair of Papa to make us stay in the wagon. I glanced sideways at Ellie. She was fussing over a box of kittens on her lap. I sighed. Ellie was all right for a sister, but she was bossy. Knowing her, she'd tell Papa for sure.

I studied the bull. It was the cause of all our trouble. Last week it had broken out twice and wandered the two miles through the bush to our farm. It bothered our cows and made Star go crazy barking, and then it trampled Ellie's lettuce and potato plants. Papa had finally made up his mind to talk to Sam Black.

"Aren't you scared?" I'd asked as we bumped along the wagon road to Sam Black's farm.

"Of course not," said Papa.

I'd thought about what my friend

Red had told me. Red's family owned the general store at The Landings. Sam Black had stopped there to pick up supplies on his way to the farm.

"Red says Sam Black's so strong he bent a piece of iron at the blacksmith's without even trying!"

"Your friend Red has a lot of imagination," said Papa.

"Red says Sam Black shot a dog between the eyes because it stole a hunk of meat off his wagon."

Papa smiled. "I don't think he'll shoot me."

I saved my best argument for the end. "Red says he heard Sam Black killed a man once and that's why everyone's so scared of him."

Papa stopped smiling then and gave me a talk about repeating gossip and judging people unfairly, and I kept quiet for the rest of the way.

Now I turned my eyes from the bull and looked hard at the cabin and hoped someone would come outside.

I wiggled on the hard wagon seat. "It's not fair," I said.

"You say that about everything," said Ellie. She lifted out a tiny, striped kitten. I looked at her face to see if she was going to cry again. Her cheeks were pale and there were puffy red circles around her eyes. In the winter, our neighbor's cat had produced a litter of kittens. They were thin and weak and only two survived. Ellie had been allowed to bring them home and nurse them until they were stronger, but now Papa said Ellie had to find homes for them at The Landings. Last night, she had cried hard and begged to keep them, but Papa said our cat Pirate was enough.

Ellie stroked the kitten, slipped it back and took out its brother. I put my hand in my pocket and touched my coin. I had earned it picking rocks in Mr. McDougall's field and as soon as we got to The Landings, I was going to spend it at the general store.

A thin plume of ragged smoke drifted

from the cabin's chimney. The windows looked cold and empty. Papa had been ages. I slid off the wagon seat and hopped to the ground.

"Get back here, Max!" said Ellie. "Papa said ..."

I pretended I didn't hear and ran through the tall weeds.

Bang! Bang!

I froze. The sound came from behind the cabin, like someone hitting something hard. I glanced up at the windows. What had happened to Papa? I sucked in my breath and ducked around the side.

A boy was swinging an axe at a log propped up against a stump. I slipped behind a tree and watched. The boy split the log in half and then picked up the pieces and threw them on a pile.

I'd never seen such a skinny boy. When he swung the axe his shoulder blades stuck out under his shirt. His feet were bare and his pants ended in a ragged line just below his knees. The boy split two more pieces of wood. Then he dropped the axe and leaned over, gulping in air, his hands on his knees.

Suddenly a door swung open at the back of the cabin, and a man burst out. Sam Black! He was much taller than Papa. He had a fierce red face, stubbly and unshaven. He wore an old undershirt and his big belly hung out between his suspenders. His arms were massive, like tree trunks, and covered with black hair.

"What do you think you're doing?" he thundered. "Ain't quitting time!"

"I wasn't ..." The boy ducked as Sam Black's huge arm swung at his back. "Ow!" He stumbled forwards and fell onto his knees.

I swallowed. I tried to stay as still as a leaf. If only I had stayed in the wagon like Papa said!

The boy stood up slowly, and for a frozen second his eyes met mine. They opened wide in surprise. His cheek was red and a thin stream of blood trickled from his nose.

I held my breath. I thought, please, please, don't give me away. Sam Black shot dogs. What would he do to a boy spying on him?

Sam Black picked up a chunk of wood. "When you're done here, you can start moving them rocks for me."

He took a long look around, his face scowling. I pressed myself against the trunk and closed my eyes. I thought he would never go. But at last I heard a grunt and the cabin door slammed shut.

I opened my eyes and peered past the tree again.

The boy wiped his face. Tears smeared the dust on his face. He glared at me. "What are you starin' at?"

My throat felt dry. I turned and ran.

Papa was climbing in the wagon. I scrambled up after him. His mouth was set in a thin tight line and he was frowning, but he didn't even seem to notice me.

Sam Black came out of the cabin and walked over to the wagon. He was smiling, like he was pleased about something. His teeth were stained brown and his beard looked dirty. He leered inside Ellie's box. "Kittens. I need some good mousers."

Ellie's shoulders tensed. She stared at Papa pleadingly.

"Well," said Papa. He looked unhappy.

Sam Black stuck his hand in the box and lifted up a kitten by the scruff of its neck. His fingernails were broken and black. He swung the kitten back and forth until it yelped. "I'll take them both."

I held my breath and didn't look at Ellie.

"No," said Papa firmly. "We're keeping the kittens actually. They're just along for the ride today."

Ellie sagged beside me. Sam Black scowled and dropped the kitten.

"Now, we'd best be going." Papa picked up the reins.

"Wait!" I said. I had spotted something glinting on the ground. My coin! It must have dropped out of my pocket. I jumped off the wagon seat and reached for the coin.

Sam Black's huge boot covered it.

I yanked my hand back. "That's my money!" I said.

"Well now, I don't think so." Sam Black leaned over and picked up the coin.

"Papa!" I cried.

Papa frowned. "Sam, my boy worked hard ..."

Sam Black smiled. "I'd call that stealin'. Coming on someone's property and takin' their money."

"Be reasonable, man," said Papa.

"I bin reasonable," said Sam Black. "I bin reasonable about my bull. I told you, if you get rid of yer cows, then my bull won't have no reason to come visiting."

He leaned towards Papa. I could smell whiskey. "Now you be reasonable and get off my property."

Silence hung between Papa and Sam Black like a thick cloud. Then Papa said, "Get in the wagon, Max."

He clucked to our horses and we bounced over the bumps and ruts.

My face burned. "Papa, that was my money! And I saw him hit his boy. He made him bleed. We ought to go back!"

Papa looked gray.

"You should do something about the boy, Papa," whispered Ellie. She pressed a kitten against her cheek. Her hands were shaking.

"And my money," I muttered.

"There's just no sense picking a fight with a man like Sam Black," said Papa. "And I can't tell a man how to raise his boy." He sounded sad.

I turned around and stared back at the cabin. Sam Black stood on the road with his fists on his hips, watching us. He laughed.

Behind him, his thin arms hugging his chest, stood the boy.

CHAPTER TWO

I saw Sam Black and his boy again a lot sooner than I wanted. By Sunday morning, Papa had finished all his business at The Landings and he and Ellie and the two kittens went home. I stayed at my Uncle Stuart's gristmill, helping him with chores and playing with Red. Our old friend Napoleon, who worked on our farm chopping trees a long time ago, was in town. He was coming back to live with us for the fall, and would bring me with him at the end of the week.

The day before we were leaving,

Napoleon and I walked up the road to the general store, so he could buy some last minute supplies. As we passed the inn, someone shouted and a loud laugh burst out. My heart jumped into my throat. I knew that mean laugh. Sure enough, Sam Black stumbled through the doorway.

I had told Napoleon all about our new neighbors. I tugged at his sleeve. "It's him," I hissed. "It's Sam Black."

A startled look crossed Napoleon's face. "So that's Sam Black," he said softly.

Before I had a chance to ask Napoleon what he meant, Sam Black swaggered across the road, his huge boots splashing right through the middle of a mud puddle, and we had to jump to get out of his way. He lurched to a stop and stared at me. He was breathing hard and his eyes were bloodshot. Then he grinned and sneered, "Spend all your money, boy?"

I clenched my fists, but Napoleon

grabbed my arm and said, "He's been drinking, Max. Just keep going."

Napoleon strode up the road, his face creased in a frown. I peeked over my shoulder once. Sam Black was bent over, shouting at a dog that slinked away with its belly low to the ground.

Napoleon had acted like he knew Sam Black. He didn't want to pick a fight with the man, just like Papa, but I didn't think it was right for everyone to run away from him. I was fuming when we went into the store. Red was hard at work, unpacking china plates from a barrel full of straw. He looked relieved to see me.

"Sam Black's in town!" I said. "And he's drunk!"

Napoleon frowned. Red glanced at the back of the store where a skinny boy stood behind a pile of bulging sugar sacks. Sam Black's boy!

The boy's cheeks flamed dark red. His eyes met mine, and I knew he remembered me. I wished I could take back my words. I looked away and pretended to be interested in a display of rakes.

Out of the corner of my eye, I watched the boy. He was wearing the same ragged pants and shirt, with a faded, red plaid cap pulled over his head. Fierce blisters covered his bare heels. Last night Uncle Stuart had told Napoleon, "If that good-for-nothing Sam Black cleared his land and planted some wheat, he'd be able to buy some food and clothes for his boy."

Two women came in the store, looking for cloth, and Red's pa spread a big bolt of brown cotton across the counter. Red swept up the straw that he'd scattered all over the floor, whistling like he always did when he finished a boring job. I helped Napoleon sort nails into a box. Papa had given me some old scraps of chicken coop lumber for the fort I was building, and I was hoping for some nails too.

Sam Black's boy poked around

nervously, peering in a few barrels. You could bet he didn't have any money. What was he doing?

Finally the boy sidled towards the door. His dirty hand hovered over a basket of lumpy brown potatoes. He grabbed one and dashed outside.

Before I could stop myself, I blurted, "Hey! He stole a potato!"

Red must have been watching him too because at the same time he yelled, "Thief!"

Everything happened fast after that.

"Come on!" hollered Red, and he dropped his broom with a clatter and ran through the door.

Behind me Napoleon said, "Wait, Max," but I raced after Red. I had to see what was going to happen.

The boy sprinted up the road, weaving through a cluster of chattering women and ducking around an ox cart.

The driver hollered, "You! Watch where you're going," but the boy kept running. For such a skinny boy, he

sure was fast. I pounded behind Red, breathing hard, as we tried to keep him in sight. The boy glanced over his shoulder and then ducked behind the blacksmith shop.

"He's going to the river," panted Red.

Behind the blacksmith's, a steep trail dropped through the forest to the river. I skidded and stumbled on the rough ground. I caught glimpses of the boy's ragged shirt and red cap through the trees, and then we slid down a bank onto the gravelly riverbed.

For a second, I thought the boy was going to plunge right into the icy water. He turned and stared wildly at us. His breath came in ragged gasps, and he still clutched the potato in his dirty hand.

I wasn't sure what Red was going to do now, and I don't think he knew either. It was so still you could hear our hearts pounding. Finally Red said, "You're a thief! Wait til my pa tells your pa."

Fear flashed across the boy's face. Then he said fiercely, "He ain't my pa."

There was a long silence. Red must have been as surprised as I was. I guess everyone figured Sam Black was the boy's pa. Finally Red said, "Then how come your name's Lucas Black?"

The boy glared at us, his eyes burning with hate, but he didn't say a word.

"You'll get a beating anyway," said Red.

"I don't care," said the boy. His voice wavered, but he met Red's eyes without flinching. Then he turned and hurled the potato into the river.

We all stared at the water. A cool breeze blew across the river, and I shivered, and hugged my arms to my chest. I was wearing my jacket with the sheepskin lining and I was cold. The boy must be freezing.

Red said, "So why don't you tell Max why you were snooping around about him? Asking questions?"

"I wasn't," said the boy.

"You were too," said Red. He turned to me. "He kept asking me how much longer you were staying in town. He was asking all kinds of nosy questions."

"I wasn't," repeated the boy.

"You're a thief *and* a liar," said Red.

The boy licked his lips. They were red and chapped, and everyone knows that licking makes them worse. Suddenly I felt a little bit sick. "Come on, Red," I muttered. "Let's leave him alone."

Red hesitated, and then said loudly, "We're just wasting our time here anyway." He sounded more disgusted than mad now.

We started back up the trail, leaving Lucas Black standing beside the river, his arms pulled tightly across his chest.

Red turned back once and shouted, "You should have kept the dumb potato."

Sam Black and Lucas must have left The Landings that day because I didn't see them again. But I couldn't stop thinking about them.

On the way home, I watched the broad backs of Napoleon's oxen as we bounced over the rough wagon road, my head whirling with confusing thoughts. Red had called the boy Lucas Black, but the boy said Sam Black wasn't his pa. And why was Lucas Black asking questions about me? Why did he care when I was coming home?

I felt better when I saw our lake through the trees. We were almost home. When Papa built our cabin, we were the only family living on the lake. Now it was hard to remember not having neighbours. We rumbled past the McDougall's farm, and I waved at Mr. McDougall and Jeremy, who were walking behind their plough in the field.

When we passed Sam Black's cabin, I turned and stared even though I didn't want to. Even more weeds had grown up in the week I'd been gone.

"I don't like Lucas Black," I said.

Napoleon turned and studied my face. "Now, why is that?"

"Well, he's a thief," I said, wishing Napoleon wouldn't stare at me quite so hard. "Nobody likes a thief."

Napoleon sighed. "He's a hungry boy. *Very* hungry, if he has to steal a potato."

I hadn't thought of that. I twisted uncomfortably on the wagon seat. I tried to think about building my fort instead. I didn't want to think about Lucas Black anymore, and I sure didn't want to have to feel sorry for him. I guess I just wished he didn't have to live with Sam Black.

CHAPTER THREE

"Sam Black was here," said Ellie.

I dropped my spoon and stared at her. "Here? When?"

"A few days ago. Papa went to the McDougall's to look at their sick horse, and I was here by myself."

"Were you scared?"

"No," said Ellie. Ellie is twelve and never admits to being scared of anything. But I bet she was.

"He walked around our fields, and he looked in everything, the henhouse and the cowshed. He had that boy with him. Then Papa came home."

I had lost all interest in my breakfast, a bowl of thick milk porridge. I shivered to think of Sam Black snooping around on our farm. "What did he want?"

"He wanted Papa to lease him a field to put some cows in," said Ellie. "But Papa said no."

She wiped her hands on her apron and reached up to a high shelf. She picked up a coin and put it on the table. "The boy said to give this to you."

The coin Sam Black had stolen from me! I stared at it in disbelief. "His name is Lucas," I said slowly. "Sam Black will kill him if he finds out."

"I told him he better not, but he said it didn't matter," said Ellie. " He said Sam Black keeps his money in an old can and by the time he figures out it's missing, he'll be gone."

"Lucas will be gone?" I repeated, surprised.

Ellie frowned. "That's what he said. He said not to tell Sam Black. He said, 'don't tell *him*,' but I knew what he meant."

Lucas Black must be pretty brave. I squirmed when I thought about chasing him through The Landings. I wish he had told me he'd given me the coin back. He hadn't said anything. He had just stared with that half-angry, half-scared look.

I shrugged away thoughts of Lucas Black and looked out the window. Napoleon had predicted a storm by afternoon, and it looked like he was right. Black clouds were building up over the lake and the water was flat and gray. Napoleon and Papa were hitching Napoleon's oxen to the plough, hoping to finish turning the new field before the storm. They had forgotten about me. Maybe I could sneak away to work on my fort.

Ellie could always read my mind. "Remember, Papa said you have to help dig potatoes before it rains," she said in a warning voice.

I sighed heavily. Normally I didn't mind digging potatoes. And I should be happy about getting my coin back. But as I followed Ellie outside to the garden, I couldn't stop worrying about Lucas Black. What did he mean, he'd be gone? Where would a boy like Lucas go?

After we finished the potatoes, Ellie went out to the barn to play with her kittens. I gathered up my nails, a hammer and an old syrup can that Napoleon had given me and headed to my fort. Our dog Star raced in front of me, tail wagging. He sped in tight circles around the henhouse and then shot down the trail into the bush, barking. Star could pick up the scent of an animal just like that, and I half expected to see a rabbit or a deer jump across the trail. But the forest was still. Why was Star acting so crazy?

My fort was in the forest behind the henhouse, beside a creek, where a huge dead tree fell over last winter. The roots pulled right out of the ground and made the back wall. My best wall was made of boards. The other two walls and the roof were made from sticks and branches, which wasn't as good because the rain came in through the holes.

I had taken Napoleon to see my fort in the morning. He said my secret trail through the bushes looked just like a deer trail and you would never know there was a fort so close. Besides Napoleon, Papa and Ellie were the only other people who knew about it. Ellie had said she would give me an old pot and a tin cup if I showed her, but I made her promise not to tell her nosy friend Kate McDougall. I did not want girls in my fort.

When we got to the fort, Star had a long drink in the creek and then plunged back into the forest, still barking. I pulled back a board and crawled inside. It felt like going into a cave, but there was enough light to see because of all the cracks in my branch walls. It was cold and smelled like wet leaves, but I liked that smell. In half of my fort you could stand straight up without bumping your head. Just before we went to The Landings, I made furniture—a bed of sacks laid over branches and a stump chair and table.

I found a good spot for the syrup can, on a kind of ledge in the roots on the back wall. A few of the sticks from my roof had fallen in, so I worked for a while repairing the holes. Muffled sounds came from outside—the tops of the trees blowing in the wind and Star barking wildly in the distance, probably at a squirrel.

After a while, I crawled back outside to check the sky. The day had got darker and the clouds right above were black. I decided to get a quick drink of water and then head home before it poured. I walked over to an old tree beside the creek, where I kept my tin cup in a hole. I stuck my hand in. The hole was empty.

I stood there for a second, confused. I had used the cup the last time I was here. I was positive I had put it back. I *always* put it back. I stared at the ground and kicked away a pile of leaves. Then I looked up and down the side of the creek. Something glinted beside a flat rock.

My cup! What was it doing over there?

I walked over and picked it up, frowning. Someone must have been here. I sucked in my breath. Ellie. She had promised not to come to the fort when I was away. But she must have come anyway! And she'd probably even brought Kate. I pictured them sitting on my chairs, using all my stuff. Resentment boiled through me.

Star's barks grew louder and then he burst out through the trees on the other side of the creek. Something that looked like a dirty red rag dangled from his mouth.

"Star!" I called. "Star! Come here! What have you got?"

Star raced up and down the side of the creek, waving his prize joyfully.

"Come!" I repeated, trying to make my voice firm like Papa's.

Finally, Star waded through the water and stood in front of me, his front legs braced to run. I pulled the rag out of his mouth. It was a wool cap.

"Star," I said slowly. "Where did you get this?"

I had seen this cap before. I frowned, thinking hard. And then I remembered.

Lucas Black, his red plaid cap darting through the trees as he ran away from us at The Landings.

My head whirled. So it wasn't Ellie at all. It was Lucas Black who had been to my fort. How had he found it?

Ellie had said that Sam Black had been at our farm when I was away. Snooping everywhere. Waiting for Papa. I remembered Ellie saying, "And he had that boy with him." I frowned. And at The Landings, Red had said that Lucas had been asking all kinds of nosy questions, wanting to know when I was coming back.

I stared across the creek. For the first time I noticed that some of the bushes were bent back, like someone had made a trail. A trail to Sam Black's cabin! It was probably no more than a mile through the forest.

My heart thumped. I had an eerie feeling that I was being watched. I strained hard to hear, but there was nothing except the sound of the wind.

Suddenly I wanted to talk to Napoleon. Napoleon would know what to do. I put my cup back in the hole in the tree and I hung the cap on a branch. Then I ran back through the forest to the henhouse.

I hurried around the side of our cabin. A huge man in big black boots stood on the porch, banging hard at the door. I froze.

Sam Black!

CHAPTER FOUR

"Hey, boy!" called Sam Black. "Come here!"

The back of my neck prickled with goosebumps. I walked slowly towards our cabin, ready to turn and run if I had to.

Sam Black spat over the railing. "Where's your papa, boy?"

I didn't say anything, but my eyes slid to the field where Napoleon and Papa were ploughing. Papa was striding towards us. He must have seen Sam Black's wagon. My legs wobbled with relief.

When Papa got close, he said, "What do you want? I told you I have no pasture to spare."

"That ain't why I'm here," said Sam Black.

"Then state your business," said Papa. "I've work to do."

This was Papa, who was never rude to visitors? I sidled closer to see what was going to happen.

"My business," said Sam Black, "is the boy. He's gone. Run away two nights ago."

Papa looked shocked. He turned to me. "Max, have you seen him?"

I slid my hand in my pocket and touched my coin. "No, sir," I said truthfully.

Something must have showed in my eyes. "Do you have any idea where he might be?"

"None," I said.

Ellie had slipped out through the door behind Sam Black. Papa nodded at her. "Ellie?"

"No, Papa."

Papa turned to Sam Black. "Then I can't help you." His voice softened. "But I hope you find the boy. I don't like to think of him out in the forest with a storm coming."

Sam Black spat again on the ground right beside Papa. Then he looked straight at me. An icy shiver ran up and down my back. I tried to stare back, but I couldn't. I dropped my eyes to the ground.

"I sure hope you ain't lyin', boy," he said softly.

"If you have something to say, say it to me," said Papa in a tight voice. "Now I told you, I have work to do."

Sam Black walked over to his wagon. He heaved his huge body onto the seat and slapped the reins across the thin gray horse's neck.

He looked at us and said, "I ain't worried about the storm. But I want the boy back. He's got a pile of work to do. I'll find him, and he'll be sorry he ever thought of running away."

Papa put his arm around Ellie and

me. The first icy drops of rain splattered on the ground as we watched Sam Black's wagon disappear around the bend in the road.

I didn't get a chance to talk to Napoleon alone. Ellie baked bread in the afternoon. We ate thick slabs with butter, watching the rain stream past the windows and listening to the rumble of thunder.

Napoleon played his fiddle for a while, and then went back to his tent to read his Bible. Papa always said we had to leave Napoleon alone when he was reading his Bible because he might be thinking about his son. Napoleon's son drowned crossing a river on a raft. For a long time we didn't know and then one day he told Papa. The other mystery about Napoleon was a big black trunk in the corner of his tent that was always locked. I wanted to ask Napoleon to open his trunk, but Papa said it was not my business.

After Napoleon left, Papa fell asleep by the fire, with a piece of half-mended harness in his hands. Ellie curled up reading. Papa had taught both Ellie and me to read, but Ellie was better at it. I sat at the table, hunched over a page of handwriting I was supposed to be copying. My mind kept jumping back to Lucas Black.

Where was he?

My eyes were drawn to the window. Tree branches lashed in the wind and the rain poured in slanted sheets over the gray lake. I shivered. What would I do if I were Lucas? Where would I go?

The fort.

I chewed my lip. I glanced at Papa, who was snoring softly. Ellie was in the other room, buried in a quilt and lost in her book. They would never know I was gone. I pushed my handwriting away and slid off the chair. Quickly, I cut a slab of bread and a chunk of cheese and wrapped them in a piece of cloth. Then I took my coat and cap off the peg and slipped outside, easing the door shut behind me.

I ran to the henhouse, my head ducked against the driving rain, and along the trail. Dripping branches slapped at my face, and my boots slipped on wet leaves. A crack of thunder made my heart jump. When I got to the creek, I hesitated, listening hard, and then I took a big breath and pulled away the board in front of my fort.

Lucas wasn't there.

Fighting back disappointment, I crawled inside. Everything was just how I left it: the sacks spread neatly over the branch bed, the syrup can, my tools. I knew he hadn't been back. I listened to the rain drumming on my stick roof and watched a puddle slowly spread across one corner of the dirt floor. I had been so sure he would come.

Where could he be?

I waited a few more minutes, then went back outside. I stared across the creek into the dark, rain-soaked trees.

I cupped my hands to my mouth and shouted, "Lucas! Lucas Black!"

Thunder crashed. I hugged my arms to my chest. "Lucas!" I hollered. "It's all right!"

Nothing. Sam Black said Lucas had run away two nights ago. He'd be awfully hungry by now. And he wouldn't have expected a storm. He must have gone back. I felt sick when I remembered the huge man's words, "He'll be sorry he ever thought about running away."

Rain ran off the edge of my cap and dripped down my neck. I couldn't stop shivering. "Lucas!" I yelled one last time, and then turned miserably to go home.

Just then something moved behind the trees. I held my breath. A second later, Lucas Black pushed his way through the clinging wet branches.

We stood still for a second, watching each other. Lucas's thin shirt was plastered to his body and his hair hung in dripping clumps over his forehead.

Then he crossed the creek, slipping from rock to rock, and stood in front of me, his dark eyes wary.

I pulled the cloth bundle out of my pocket. It was slightly squashed but dry.

"I brought you something," I said.

CHAPTER FIVE

"I only stayed here at night," Lucas said between mouthfuls of bread and cheese. "And I never took anything."

He sat hunched over on the stump chair, tearing the bread into chunks and cramming it into his mouth. I stared at him. His face went red and he muttered, "My food ran out yesterday."

"I can bring more." I blurted the question that was burning inside me. "How did you find my fort?"

Lucas swallowed. "Easy! We came to your farm once when you were away. Anyone could see that trail behind the henhouse went somewhere, so I followed it to see. And then I had to figure out how to get here from my place. I came along the creek."

I had been pretty sure my fort was well hidden and I felt annoyed, but I had something even more important to ask. "Does Sam Black know about it?"

"Well I ain't *that* dumb!" said Lucas scornfully.

We sat in silence while Lucas finished off the last of the cheese.

Something scratched on the branches outside my fort. Lucas stiffened, but then a whining sound made me laugh. "It's just Star," I said. I pushed back the board. "Get in here, boy."

Star wiggled joyfully to see me and then shook all over, spraying us with water. For the first time I saw Lucas smile. "Guess I can't get any wetter anyway." He bent down and rubbed Star's ears.

"I had a dog," he said suddenly. "He drowned it."

I swallowed. "Is Sam Black your uncle?"

"No! He ain't no kin of mine. He married my ma, but that don't make him kin."

Lucas looked up at me and his words spilled out. "I had a pa, but he died when I was a baby. Ma had all kinds of jobs and then she got a job for *him*, cooking and looking after his house. He married her so he wouldn't have to pay her. He just wanted a servant."

I pulled Star close to me and hugged his damp body. "Why did your ma agree to marry him?"

Lucas shrugged. "She thought it would be better for me, on account of she wasn't strong and it was getting harder and harder for her to work. And he wasn't so bad at first. But we didn't need him! I had a job, selling newspapers, and I had a whole can of money saved for Ma and me. He stole it from me, but I aim to get it back one day. It's *my* money!"

"Where's your ma now?" I asked.

"She's dead," said Lucas flatly. "We were living in New York, but there was trouble. He came home one night and said we had to leave. We went to Montreal and then Ma got really sick and died. That's when he drowned my dog."

I thought about that for a minute. Napoleon had told Papa he'd spent last winter in Montreal. I wondered if that's where he'd run into Sam Black before.

"My mama's dead too," I said finally. "She died in England before we came to Canada." Lucas looked sympathetic and I added truthfully, "I don't really miss her 'cause I don't remember her."

"I miss my ma," said Lucas simply. "I think about her every day so I won't forget what she looks like. She had a locket with her picture in it. I'd never forget her if I had the locket, but *he* sold it."

I wanted to ask a pile more questions, like what kind of trouble did Sam Black get into in New York, but

I decided I better stop. Ellie always said I was too nosy.

For the first time, I noticed how quiet it had become outside. I hopped off my stump and pushed back the board and peered outside. "Storm's over. Come on, Lucas."

We stood beside the fort for a few minutes, watching water drip from the leaves. It had stopped raining and the clouds were breaking up in the sky. Lucas shivered.

"I'll go get you some dry clothes and some more food," I said. "I'll be right back."

"Can you leave Star?" said Lucas.

"Sure."

He grabbed my arm. "Don't tell anyone I'm here."

"I won't," I said.

"Swear."

"I swear."

"Double swear on our mothers' graves."

I didn't think Papa would approve, but I said, "Double swear."

Lucas dropped my arm and I ran.

When I got back to the cabin, Papa and Napoleon were in the field and Ellie was in the barn with her kittens. I bundled together a pair of pants and a shirt and some more bread and cheese and took them back to the fort. Lucas was fast asleep, rolled up in a sack on my branch bed. I left the food and clothes on the ground beside him, whistled for Star, who had wandered away into the forest, and then went home.

For the rest of the day I hugged my secret to myself. Papa had left a pile of firewood for me to stack and I had water buckets to fill and the horses to feed. I was tired when Ellie called Papa and Napoleon and me in for supper.

We ate in silence for a while. Napoleon swallowed his thick slab of ham in two bites, a feat which usually impressed me, but this time my mind was too busy to watch. I poked at my piece of cornbread and thought about Lucas. Did he trust me? How long could he stay in my fort? What would happen if Sam Black found him?

We were just starting on apple cake when someone banged on our door. It was our neighbor, Jeremy McDougall, Kate's older brother. He accepted a huge piece of cake and then talked quickly with his mouth full. "Sam Black was at our place this morning."

"He was here too," said Papa.

"He's been up and down the lake to everybody's farms," said Jeremy. He brushed crumbs from his mouth. "Looking for his boy. My pa says we should put together a search party if the boy's not back by morning."

"A good idea," said Papa. He looked at Napoleon and Napoleon nodded. "Tell your pa to count Napoleon and me in."

My heart pounded. "Maybe he doesn't want to be found. He's not lost. He ran away. That's different."

Papa gave me a searching look and

I stared down at the table. Then he said slowly, "Whether he wants to be found or not, he's just a boy. The nights are cold and there's wild animals."

"You can't make him go back to Sam Black's, Papa!" said Ellie. Her face was white.

Papa sighed. "I told you before, I can't interfere with how a man raises his son."

"That's not fair," said Ellie.

"And he's not his son," I cried. "He's not even kin!"

Everyone stared at me and my cheeks went hot. "He told me that at The Landings," I muttered. "His ma married Sam Black, but he's not blood kin!"

Jeremy shifted uncomfortably and said, "I don't know about that. But my pa says everyone should check their barns and cowsheds. He could be hiding anywhere." He eyed the last slice of cake, but Ellie pretended not to see.

"I'll do that now, before it gets dark," said Papa. He stood up. I pushed back my chair and Papa added, "Max, I see that handwriting is still waiting to be done. I want you in the cabin working tonight."

I stayed at the table until everyone had gone and Ellie had her back turned, scrubbing fiercely at a pan. I knew Ellie would stay mad at Papa all night. Quickly, I grabbed two chunks of cornbread and slid them in my pocket.

I slumped over my handwriting, my mind spinning. A search party! How long would it be before Papa thought of the fort?

CHAPTER SIX

I tossed in my bed in the loft, thinking about Lucas. Our cat Pirate jumped with a thump onto my stomach. I reached down and pulled him up to my face. I hugged his warm body and listened to his soft purring.

Yip! Yip! Yip! Somewhere in our field coyotes sang. Pirate stiffened, squeezed out of my arms and thudded to the floor. I was used to the noise, but it still sent tingles up my spine. Lucas must be listening to them too. Was he scared?

I climbed out of bed and went downstairs. I scooped a drink of water from the bucket and stood by the window. Papa and Napoleon were on the porch, their pipes glowing in the dark. The door was open a crack and snatches of their voices drifted through.

Papa said, "I'll paddle across to the Indian camp ... long way, but he might have gone that far."

And then I heard Napoleon's soft voice, "... not fit to raise a boy ... trouble in New York ... I knew I'd seen him before ..."

I slipped closer to the door, straining to hear.

Papa murmered something and Napoleon said, "... in the tavern in Montreal ... I heard him talking ..."

The coyotes burst into a new song, and it was hard to hear. I caught part of Naopleon's voice, "... man was dead ... Sam Black left New York in a hurry ..."

I gasped out loud. Silence fell on the porch. Then Papa coughed and pushed the door shut.

The back of my neck prickled. I didn't care if Papa knew I was listening. So, everything Red said was true. Sam Black *had* killed a man. Legs shaking, I went back upstairs to my bed.

Sam Black was a murderer! I tried to remember Papa's exact words when Ellie said, "You can'---t make him go back to Sam Black's!" He had said something about not interfering. After hearing Napoleon, would Papa still think that? I pulled my thick quilt up to my neck, but I stayed icy cold.

I decided to stay awake all night so I could get up early, before Papa. I had to warn Lucas!

Men's voices drifted up through my window in the loft. Blinking from sleep, I crawled out of bed and peered outside. The morning was foggy, but I could see the shapes of men gathered at the side of the road: Papa and Mr. McDougall and Jeremy and two farmers who lived at the end of the lake. The search party! I had slept in!

The men faded away in the fog. I hurried downstairs. Ellie was still asleep. Hastily, I laid a cloth on the table and filled it with pieces of bread and ham from last night's supper. I rolled it up tightly, grabbed my coat and dashed outside.

Thump! I bumped straight into Napoleon who was coming in the door. I dropped my bundle, and bread and ham scattered everywhere. He stepped back while I gathered up the food, my cheeks blazing.

"My breakfast," I stammered. "I'm going to help look for Lucas and I didn't have time to eat. The search party has gone already."

Napoleon nodded. He stared thoughtfully at the bundle of food clutched in my hands. He said, "I went out early. I couldn't sleep thinking about the boy. He'll be mighty hungry by now."

I squirmed. Finally Napoleon said,

"I'm going to grab a mug of coffee."

I waited until he had shut the door and then ran to the henhouse. I looked back once and sucked in my breath. There was a shadow at the window and I was sure I saw someone move. Then the window was empty. I sped down the trail to my fort.

Lucas was awake and hungry. He ate eagerly while I talked. "You can't stay here. There's a search party looking for you. Papa will think of the fort; I know he will. And they'll make you go back to Sam Black."

Lucas stopped chewing. "I'm never going back there," he said. "I'm going to New York."

My mouth dropped. "What?"

Lucas swallowed. "I been thinking about it all night. I got friends in New York. And I can get my old job back, selling newspapers. I know I can. I just got to get to The Landings without him catching me. Then I can get a stage- coach to Montreal."

I stared at Lucas admiringly. "What would you do after that?"

For a second Lucas looked uncertain, then he shrugged. "I'll think of something. Maybe I'll hide on a ship sailing to New York."

We were both silent for a few minutes, Lucas chewing and me thinking hard. Then I said slowly, "Some lum-bermen have a camp a couple of miles past our farm. They've been cutting down trees for weeks. They must be ready to take a log boom to The Landings any day now. One of the men is my friend Pierre. He'll take you."

Lucas looked wary. "Can you trust him?"

"Yes," I said.

"And you won't tell anybody else I'm here?"

"I told you, I swear!" I said. But I felt uneasy when I remembered the thoughtful look on Napoleon's face when he looked at my bundle of food and the shadow at the window.

Lucas relaxed. "Okay."

I jumped up. "I'll go now. I'll be back as soon as I can."

I ran down the trail, my head buzzing with plans, when suddenly a man's voice made me skid to a stop. I froze, shrinking back into the trees.

Napoleon and Sam Black were standing beside the henhouse.

"He's hidin' here somewhere," said Sam Black. "That boy here knows something."

I swallowed hard.

"I told you, he's not here," said Napoleon. "And I told you to get off this farm."

"I ain't goin' til I get the boy." Sam Black swung his arm, and I saw he was holding a brown bottle.

"You won't find him here," said Napoleon evenly. Despite my fear, a thrill spread through me. Napoleon didn't sound scared of Sam Black at all.

Then Sam Black stared straight at the trees where I was hiding. I was

close enough to see the black stubble on his face and his mean bloodshot eyes. "Well now, I figure someone's been going back and forth here," he said. "Think I'll take a look around."

"It's a deer trail," said Napoleon. "It doesn't go anywhere. And I've searched all around here anyway. There's no sign of Lucas."

Papa always said that Napoleon was as truthful as the day was long. And he had just lied to Sam Black! I shivered.

Sam Black took a swig from his bottle. "I always said to his ma the boy was no good. I'll whip him when I find 'im."

Napoleon's face tightened. "I told you to get off this farm."

"Get off the farm," Sam Black mimicked in a sneering voice. He dropped the bottle and it smashed on a rock.

I sucked in my breath, trying to steady my pounding heart. Then I heard distant voices, Papa calling to someone, and a horse whinnying. Relief flooded through me. Papa and the men were back!

Sam Black turned his head and scowled. Then he said, "I'm goin', cause I got things to do. But I'll be back. I want that boy."

I watched Napoleon follow Sam Black towards our cabin. I stayed in the trees a long time, until I heard Sam Black's wagon rumble down the road.

Then I set off at a run for the logging camp.

CHAPTER SEVEN

"Pierre!" I shouted.

My voice echoed through the empty camp. I pushed open the door of the long, log shanty where the lumbermen lived. Bunks lined the walls, with neat bedrolls at each end, and wool pants, coats and hats hung on nails. A leftover smell of woodsmoke and roasted meat hung in the air. But there were no men.

I went back outside and looked at the lake. My heart sank. I was too late. A huge log boom floated on the water, farther from shore than I could yell. The lumbermen paddled along the side in their big birch canoes, and two men stood on the log boom, holding long poles. I recognized Pierre.

He saw me standing on the shore and waved and shouted something, but I couldn't hear.

"Come back!" I hollered. "Please, Pierre! Come back!"

Pierre smiled and waved again. My shoulders slumped as they moved slowly down the lake. They were paddling towards a point of land, covered with blueberry bushes, that formed the end of the bay. Ellie and I had named it Blueberry Point, and we walked there in the summer to pick berries. It was about a mile from our farm.

When the lumbermen passed Blueberry Point, they would be close to shore, maybe close enough to hear me. If I ran hard, I could beat them there! I raced back down the trail towards home, my heart pounding in my chest, and veered off on our well-worn path to

Blueberry Point. After a few minutes I broke out of the forest. I pushed through the blueberry bushes, branches swiping my face and pulling at my clothes, until I was at the shore.

"Pierre!" I hollered.

The lumbermen had passed the point and were heading out to the middle of the lake. I picked up a rock and hurled it at the water.

Pierre waved his pole in the air and shouted, "See you in a week!" Then the lumbermen burst into one of their lively French songs.

With a huge sigh, I waved back. I watched them until they were just a speck down the lake and their songs had faded away. The lumbermen would be back to cut more trees and build another log boom. But they wouldn't go to The Landings again until next month.

Lucas couldn't wait that long.

I walked home, looking fearfully at the road in front of our cabin for Sam Black's wagon. But the road was empty.

Ellie was hanging some washing on the clothesline. "Is Papa back yet?" I called.

"Not yet," said Ellie. "Come and help me."

I passed up wet shirts while Ellie clipped them to the line. All the time she worked, she talked about how mean Sam Black was and how she hoped he never got Lucas back. Then Ellie went inside and I slumped down on the porch step. How could I tell Lucas that the lumbermen had left without him? That I had been too late!

A plume of smoke drifted from the stovepipe sticking out through the top of Napoleon's tent. He knows, I thought. He knows Lucas is in the fort and he didn't tell. I jumped off the step and ran to Napoleon's tent and called loudly, "Napoleon? Are you home?"

"Come in, Max," said Napoleon, and I pulled back the canvas flap. I loved Napoleon's tent and wanted to live in one just like it some day. It had wooden boxes for his things, a tin stove, his mysterious black trunk and even a bed.

I stared in surprise, forgetting for a second all about Lucas. Napoleon was kneeling beside the trunk and the lid was open! Finally I could see what was inside. I peered over his shoulder eagerly and then blinked with disappointment. There were no treasure or bones or old maps or anything exciting. The trunk was full of clothes!

Napoleon smiled at the look on my face. He lifted out a thick, wool jacket and held it up. "This belonged to my son, Noah," he said. His voice was matter-of-fact, but his hands shook. I knelt beside him.

"Were all these clothes Noah's?" I asked.

"Yes," said Napoleon. "I put everything in here when he drowned." He held up a pair of pants. "He was a little older than you, but he wasn't very big."

I looked into the trunk and spotted something shiny tucked into the clothes. "Oh, look, Napoleon!" I said, pulling out a thin metal harmonica.

Without thinking I played a few notes. I stopped, stricken, when I saw Napoleon's ashen face. "I'm sorry," I stammered.

"No one has played it since Noah," said Napoleon.

"I'm sorry," I repeated. I would have given anything to take that sad look off Napoleon's face. I put the harmonica back in the trunk and watched while Napoleon sorted through thick socks, a fur-lined cap and a wool shirt.

I swallowed. "Napoleon," I said, my words coming out in a rush. "Lucas needs to get to The Landings before Sam Black finds him. I tried to see if Pierre would take him, but I was too late. They'd gone already. I ran all the way."

I stopped talking and waited, my heart pounding.

Napoleon said softly, "I can't take

a boy away from his father, Max. That would be kidnapping."

"He's not his father!" I said desperately.

Napoleon sighed. "His stepfather, then. I'm afraid it would be the same thing in the eyes of the law. But I can try to talk to Sam Black."

"It won't do any good!" I said. "Please Napoleon! Just to The Landings!"

"I can't, Max." Napoleon put his hand on my arm, but I pushed him away. I stood up.

"Take him the jacket and the hat," said Napoleon. "It's getting so cold at night."

I looked at Napoleon for a long time, then I took the clothes. "Thank you," I muttered.

Napoleon and I went outside. I felt him watching me as I walked away.

"Max!" he called.

I turned around slowly.

"I'm thinking that I should take a trip to The Landings tomorrow, but there'll be no room for passengers. The back of my wagon will be full of sacks. Potatoes and grain." He gave me a long hard look. "Do you understand?"

I stared at Napoleon, then a smile spread across my face.

"I'm leaving early," said Napoleon. "Before it's light. I'm loading the sacks tonight."

I nodded and then I broke into a run, Noah's clothes pressed tight against my chest.

CHAPTER EIGHT

"I can't go until I get my money," said Lucas.

I stared at Lucas, horrified. He was sitting on a stump in the fort, huddled in the warmth of Noah's wool coat. His face looked pale and ghostly in the fading afternoon light.

"He'll kill you if you go back," I said finally.

"I'll sneak in," said Lucas bravely. "When he's asleep. I have to. It's my money, and I need it for New York."

I fell silent, my head spinning. Lucas was right. I was sure Napoleon would take him to The Landings, but without money, he'd be stuck there. And Sam Black would find him for sure.

Lucas said, "The money's in a can under the floor. There's a loose board. I'll just take what's mine."

I shivered. "He'll wake up."

"No, he won't," said Lucas flatly. "He drinks all afternoon and then he climbs up into the loft and stays there until morning. It's always the same."

I shuddered. How horrible it must have been for Lucas. It seemed forever ago that I had told Napoleon that I didn't like Lucas Black.

I took a deep breath. "I'll come with you."

Lucas looked at me for a long time. Then he licked his lips and stood up. "We better go now."

We followed the creek through the forest to Sam Black's cabin. We didn't talk. It was almost dark when we got there, and I worried that Ellie would be calling me for supper. I pushed the thought out of my head. I would tell Papa everything once Lucas was safe. Papa would understand.

Lucas and I hid in the trees at the edge of the clearing, studying the cabin. The thin gray horse stared at us, and I held my breath, afraid it would whinny and give us away. But after a long look, it lowered its head and picked at the scraggly grass in its pen.

"Someone ought to feed that horse," I muttered.

"No hay," said Lucas flatly. He touched my arm. "Shh. Listen."

There was a thumping sound and the door of the cabin swung open. Sam Black filled the doorway, scowling into the night. Lucas and I shrank back deeper into the trees.

Sam Black laughed, a loud mean laugh that ran down my back like ice. "I know you're out there, boy!" he yelled.

For a second, I thought he had seen us, but then his eyes swung wildly from side to side. I tried not to breathe, to stay as still as I possibly could.

Then the door slammed, and my knees wobbled.

"We have to wait now," said Lucas shakily. He sat down on the end of a log. I sat beside him, rubbing my arms to get warm and to stop my teeth from chattering. A candle flickered in the cabin window. I watched it for a long time.

For a while, Lucas and I whispered together. Lucas told me about New York, and I tried to imagine the huge crowds and the tall buildings and the ships in the harbour. Then Lucas was quiet. I shifted, easing a cramp out of my leg.

I tried to think of good things like Ellie and supper and our cabin. I thought of Napoleon loading the sacks in the wagon, leaving a space for Lucas.

There was a thud near the cabin, and Lucas and I both jumped, but it was only a squirrel dropping pinecones.

It was so dark now that I couldn't see the horse, but I could hear him moving restlessly in the shadows.

After a long time, Lucas said, "I think I can get it now."

I stared at the dark cabin, my heart thumping. "The candle ... "

"He must have left it burning. I know him. He'll be asleep for sure by now. Come on."

We ran across the clearing. I stepped on a branch and the crack sounded as loud as a gunshot. I was terrified that any second Sam Black would come charging out after us. We crouched under the window for a minute, catching our breath, then Lucas peered through the dark glass. He gave a low grunt. "I told you, he's gone to bed. And there's enough candle left to see by."

We slipped over to the door. Lucas stood there for a minute, breathing hard. Then he eased it open. It gave a low creak, and I held my breath. Lucas froze. I peered over his shoulder into the dark cabin, my spine tingling with fear. The candle was on the middle of a table, just a stub left, sputtering in a pool of wax. A sour sweaty smell made me wrinkle my nose. In the flickering light I could see a few more pieces of furniture—an old dresser and some chairs and a thin mat in the corner with a blanket spread across it, which must have been where Lucas slept.

Then I saw Sam Black, his huge body crumpled in a heap at the bottom of a rickety ladder.

Lucas gasped.

"He's dead," I said.

Just then Sam Black rolled his head back. His eyes opened and he let out a long moan.

"Run!" yelled Lucas. "Run!"

CHAPTER NINE

"Help!" called Sam Black.

Lucas and I froze outside the door. My heart was pounding so hard I thought my chest would burst. Sam Black's voice was thin and weak, but it still sent chills down my back.

"Help!" he called again.

The moon had slipped out through the clouds, and the clearing around the cabin and the road were bathed in light. Napoleon's wagon must be ready by now, loaded with sacks of potatoes, with a small space left for Lucas. It was Lucas's only chance to

get away. The plan had seemed per-
fect. More than anything I wanted to
run down that road for home.

But Sam Black was lying inside the
cabin, badly hurt, maybe even dying.

I braced myself. "I'll stay," I said.
"You go to our cabin and get Papa."

Lucas acted as if he didn't hear me
and I gave his arm a rough push. "Go,
Lucas! Go on the road. You have to!"

Lucas shuddered, like he was going to be sick. Then he turned and
ran. I waited until I couldn't see him
anymore. I took a deep breath and
went back inside the cabin.

Sam Black grunted when he saw
me. "Ever see a man die?" he mumbled, and fear flashed in his eyes.

"No!" My voice sounded high and
frightened. His leg was bent at a strange
angle. I swallowed. "What should I do?"

Sam Black closed his eyes. His face
was gray and beads of sweat glistened
on his forehead. For a long time, he
didn't answer and I thought he was

dead for sure. Then his body started to shake violently and he said, "Water ... I need some water."

I took a cup from a clutter of dirty dishes on the table and filled it from a bucket by the door. Slowly I stepped towards Sam Black. I set the cup on the floor beside him. He eased himself up on an elbow and took a few long gulps.

He leaned back and shut his eyes again. His body shook. I grabbed the blanket off the mat on the floor. It was dirty and thin, but I couldn't see anything else. I laid the blanket over his huge body, trying not to look at his leg. I thought I would throw up if he opened his eyes and looked at me.

I moved back against the door. I swallowed. Papa! Please come, Papa! Lucas was a fast runner. I remembered how fast he had run through The Landings when we chased him. How long would it take him to get Papa?

Sam Black's voice made me jump.

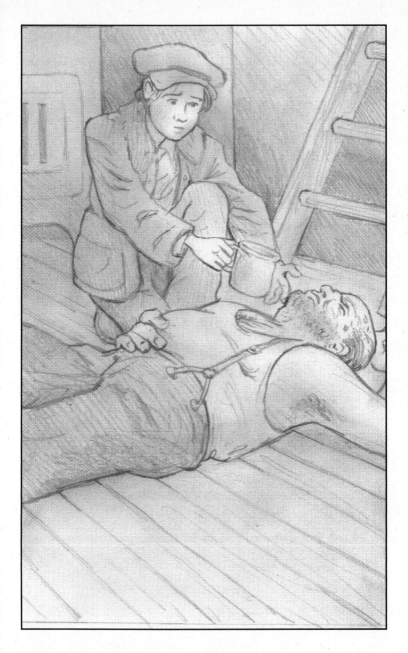

"In the dresser. Top right ... "

Reluctantly, I stepped closer. "What's in the dresser?" I asked.

"Painkiller," whispered the man. "Brown bottle."

My hands shaking, I pulled open a drawer and fumbled through a clutter of candles stubs, strips of leather, a knife ... no bottle. Behind me, Sam Black moaned. My hands touched something smooth and hard, wrapped in a piece of cloth. I picked it up and a small silver heart on a chain, dull with tarnish, fell into my hand. The locket! Sam Black hadn't sold it after all! Forgetting for a second about the man, I snapped the locket open. Inside was a faded picture of a woman. Lucas's mother.

"That's mine," said Sam Black icily. "Leave it alone."

My heart lurched. His eyes bored into my back. I dropped the locket in the drawer.

"I said ... the ... *right* drawer." Sam

Black gasped for breath between each word. I pulled open the right drawer and spotted the brown bottle. I took the lid off and then handed it to Sam Black. I watched with a mixture of fascination and horror as he poured some into his mouth. He grimaced, and brown liquid dribbled on his chin.

He looked at me once and said, "You afraid of me, boy?"

"No!" I said.

Then he gave a huge groan and his head dropped back down on the floor. His cheeks had a strange gray sheen and his huge body shook right through the thin blanket.

Please, please don't die until Papa gets here, I whispered to myself. I didn't want to be alone in the cabin with a dead man.

I put a chair beside the door and sat on it. I was afraid to open it, in case the cold air made Sam Black die even faster, so I had to keep jumping up to look out the window. For the first time I noticed that the candle had burned out, but there was enough moonlight coming through the window to see. After what seemed like forever, Papa galloped up the road on our horse, George.

I ran outside. I wanted Papa to pull me into his arms and hug me tight, but he just gave me a quick word, "Are you all right, son?" and when I said, "Yes," he pushed past me into the cabin.

Shivering, I followed Papa. He wrinkled his nose at the smell and then he stood over Sam Black. He pulled back the blanket and grunted and then covered him up again.

"Is he dead yet?" I whispered.

A ghost of a smile crossed Papa's face. He said, "No, and he's not going to die. But he's got a badly broken leg and he's in shock." Papa put his arm on my shoulder. "You were brave, Max. You did the right thing. The blanket was a good idea. It's important to keep him warm."

Then Papa leaned over Sam Black and said, "You're going to be fine. Napoleon has gone for the doctor."

I couldn't bear to be in the cabin any longer and I went outside to wait for Napoleon. After a long time I heard hooves and Napoleon trotted up on our horse, Billy. A few minutes later, the doctor's wagon rattled into the yard.

The doctor dropped the reins and jumped down. He gave me a concerned look and then went inside. After a few minutes, I heard Sam Black shout out in pain and I put my hands over my ears.

Finally Papa came outside. "The doctor says he wants you home and in bed." He scooped me up and put me on George. Then he swung up into the saddle in front of me.

"Why did Sam Black yell?" I asked.

"The doctor set his leg," said Papa. "He'll be all right now. The doctor and Napoleon will stay for a while."

I took a big breath. "Lucas?"

"We'll talk about Lucas tomorrow," said Papa in a firm voice.

I rested my head against Papa's back and tried to still the fear in my chest. Would Papa make Lucas go back to Sam Black? I wished tomorrow would never come.

CHAPTER TEN

Lucas slept beside me in my bed in the loft. He tossed and turned, and it was a long time before I could get to sleep. Once, in the middle of the night, Lucas sat straight up and called out something. In the morning his face was white with black smudges under his eyes.

We ate breakfast in silence. Each mouthful stuck in my throat. I kept looking at the empty spot where Napoleon usually sat and then at Papa, but he avoided my eyes.

After the meal, I followed Papa outside. "You can't let Sam Black have Lucas.

Sam Black is a murderer!"

Papa was walking to the barn. He stopped and turned around. His face was dark, and I added nervously, "It's true! I heard Napoleon telling you. Sam Black left New York because a man was killed."

Papa gave me a long hard look. "Sam Black says he and the man had argued over some money, but nothing more. He left New York because he was afraid he might be falsely accused."

My face felt hot and Papa added sternly, "I suggest if you're going to listen in on conversations, you listen to the whole thing before you form your opinions."

I waited until Papa had gone and then muttered, "That's what Sam Black *says*."

I thought the day would never end. After supper, Ellie and Lucas and I played in the barn with the kittens.

"You can pick one for yourself, Lucas," said Ellie generously.

Lucas's face brightened and then a cloud passed over his eyes. I wondered if he was thinking about his dog that

Sam Black had drowned. "Maybe I will," he mumbled.

There was a dull feeling in my stomach and after a while I left Lucas and Ellie and went outside. I sat on the cabin step and whittled a piece of wood with my knife. I could hear Papa restlessly moving around inside the cabin. My eyes kept looking up, straining down the road to Sam Black's cabin.

Suddenly the clop of hooves rang through the darkness and Napoleon came around the bend in the road, riding Billy and leading Sam Black's thin gray horse behind him. I jumped up.

"Papa," I yelled. "Papa, Napoleon's back."

Papa stepped out through the door behind me. Napoleon rode up to the cabin. I bit my lip to hold back the questions bursting inside me.

Naopleon looked tired. He climbed down off Billy and wiped his brow with his hand. He nodded at Papa. "Sam Black sold me the horse. He's going to give up farming and look for work in Montreal."

I sucked in my breath. Montreal! Papa didn't seem at all surprised. "I never saw a man less suited to farming," he said. "When is he planning on leaving?"

"As soon as his leg is fit to travel. I offered to take him as far as The Landings in a few days."

"Good," said Papa.

I should have been happy that Sam Black wasn't going to be our neighbor for much longer, but all I could think about was Lucas.

Then Papa said, "And the boy ... "

I went still inside.

Napoleon cleared his throat. "Turns out Sam Black never legally adopted Lucas. He figures the boy will be a nuisance now he's leaving the farm."

"Well?" said Papa. I looked at him in surprise. Papa sounded as bursting to know as me.

"I'm planning on taking Lucas to

live with me," Napoleon said in a rush. "That is, if he agrees."

"He will!" I shouted. "I'm going to tell him right now!"

Papa grabbed my arm. "I think Napoleon can handle that by himself," he said with a smile.

"One strange thing," said Napoleon. He reached into his pocket and took out the silver locket. "Sam Black gave me this. He said to give it to Lucas."

"There's a picture of Lucas's mother in it," I said slowly. "Sam Black said it was his."

"Well, I guess he changed his mind," said Papa. He put his arm around me. "We'll never really understand a man like Sam Black."

"Napoleon!" cried Ellie, and we all turned to watch Ellie and Lucas running up from the barn. Lucas still clutched one of the kittens to his chest.

"Ellie, I need you in the house," called Papa. He turned to me and added firmly, "And you too, Max."

Papa lit the lamp and read to Ellie and me. It was hard to listen to the story. I kept popping up to go to the door. I strained to see what was happening down at Napoleon's tent. Napoleon and Lucas were two black shadows against the firelight, and the murmer of voices drifted to the cabin. Did Lucas still want to go to New York? Napoleon was older than Papa and sometimes he read his Bible all night without talking. Would Lucas mind?

Then I heard a new sound, a sound which made a tingle run up my spine.

I said, "Papa, Ellie, Lucas is staying! Come here quickly."

They hurried out to the step beside me.

"What is it?" said Ellie.

"Shh," I said. "Listen."

Ellie shivered, and Papa put his arms around both of us and pulled us close. For a long time we heard nothing.

And then through the still night came the joyful notes of a harmonica.

In the fourth volume of her historical series set in Upper Canada in the 1830s, BECKY CITRA tackles the serious subject of abuse while staying true to her characters and telling a gripping story. In addition to the Max and Ellie stories, Becky is also the author of *Dog Days* (Orca, 2003) a hilarious story about a boy who must overcome his fear of dogs in order to make friends in a new town.

A primary school teacher and writer, Becky Citra lives on a ranch in Bridge Lake, B.C., where horses, bears and coyotes abound and where many of the chores have not changed since Max's day.